EGGSHELL EXPRESSION

ISBN: 978-1-7359803-4-8

EGGSHELL EXPRESSION

J. EVERETT DUTSCHKE

THIS THESIS OUTLINES AND deals with what I believe to be an unnecessary and obstructive boundary issued by the CBT community to curb my (Dutschke) ability to properly express myself.

My methodology, which depends on precision of expressed cognition, must not only be accepted, but should be adopted by other team leaders, therapists, counselors, and staff psychologists as a matter of course.

History

ON NUMEROUS OCCASIONS, INDIVIDUAL community members and staff have criticized my syntax and strongly advised me to "remember my audience," in essence, suggesting that others cannot understand me—implying then that they cannot "help me."

This has occurred following my "pull up" microphone responses (three times), in pre-journal groups, process group, and on documentary tools—all repeatedly. Among those have been A. Lopez, Sickles, Mr. Green, Spiotto, Cavna, Arsenault, J. Davis, Alverado, Dillon, Hassan, Clark, Bell, Candra, Walker, Rose, MacArthur, Reczko, Oreccio, Mungia, and... well, practically everyone else.

The expectation placed on me then has been the undue (and I maintain *improper*) strictures on my expression to articulate only to the lowest perceived common denominator (a metric that I believe should be horribly insulting to others) of "the audience" (which presumably implies not merely the least adept with nuance of language in the room, but also any individual reviewing or assessing any documentary tool—i.e. attitude checks, RSAs, etc.). This is not only a difficult task, it is near impossible, to say the least. And it is unreasonable.

Here's why:

I am deliberate and precise with my speech by design and on purpose. Speech—written or spoken—is our sole tool of accurate cognitive expression. While true that some occasions call for vague, undetailed expression, most every other occasion (especially any clinical matter) calls instead for precision.

By education, I am a physiologist, (I minored in psychology

as well). Imagine, if you will, if I was monitoring my bank of a cardiac patient's telemetries and I called the patient's cardiologist in the middle of the night to report to the doctor in vague terms, "Doctor, Mrs. Smith's heart is acting funny." Of course, such an asinine report would demand the reply, "Well, what exactly is it doing?"

Now imagine if I was forbidden from expressing to him the details, which can be very nuanced, and could only give him vague outlines. Such a report would give him nothing on which to act, therefore nothing on which to base any accurate or customized treatment. He could then order some cookie-cutter response, but that would be unthinkable and improper. Mrs. Smith's life is (and often was) at stake and depends on precise language.

A proper analysis of that patient's telemetry would detail the issue in full, and without strictures on syntax:

"The patient had several sporadic PVCs which gained in frequency. Her telemetric history shows progression to atrial tachycardia or even v-tach prior to stroke. Her blood pressure dropped concurrently. This (reporting) episode began at 11:53 p.m. and lasted until 12:15 a.m. Her respirations increased and O2 saturation fell to 92% just before she entered 23 seconds of atrial fibrillation, which then stabilized into a normal sinus rhythm at 92 bpm, with a prolonged QT interval and peaked P waves."

Now this analysis would give the doctor something more to treat than simply "her heart isn't acting right. It is struggling with responsibility and objectivity." ("Well, give Mrs. Smith an attitude check and call me in the morning.")

Even during my clinical rotations (including my psych rotations), I was taught that care plans and even overall treatment plans required accurate assessments (questions and analysis) based on accurate and precise reporting by the patient themselves. Thus, precise language is important, no, *imperative*, all the way down to *EVERY* level.

Imagine a suspected case of appendicitis:

"Where exactly does it hurt?"

"I dunno, my torso."

Is that precision adequate to then perform an appendectomy? Of course not. Suboptimal language will lead to suboptimal results. Maybe the pain is actually diverticulitis, gall bladder infection, a tumor. Maybe she has an impaction or maybe it's just gas. Will yanking out her appendix (which, these days, is pretty much a routine, cookie-cutter solution) help?

Of course not.

Therefore...

I. The precision of language is a key element in the very diagnosis itself.

LIKEWISE, TREATMENT (IN THE relevant parallel, here delivered as "feedback") of the clinical issue must also be precise. (Yes, I said "must." Don't panic.)

Even if the diagnosis is correct, the exactness and precision of the tool must not be compromised. Yes, an appendectomy probably could be performed with a sledgehammer instead of a scalpel, but... really... what a mess.

(Please ignore that in current times, not even scalpels are used for appendectomies, as they are now even more precise, and "scoped.")

My obvious point is the elementary and axiomatic truth that the depth of analysis can only be expressed properly with its commensurate depth of language.

While I will show later in this paper that the inverse is equally true—that analytical depth actually *REQUIRES* commensurate language even *BEFORE* the step of expression—this bears repeating:

> The depth of analysis can only be properly expressed with a commensurate depth of language.

Because of the conditions, introspection being the core and primary tactic for gathering information, every single step of the treatment/elevation cycle is necessarily contingent upon the step before it. Which means that any failure at the initial stage—in this case, introspection (information gathering)—will permeate every other stage, causing an inexorable and catastrophic target shift at its furthest projection (treatment and revelation of treatment). That is, any variance at the point of origin, however small, is self-amplified incrementally to be far off target. In other words, an inch off at the rifle's barrel here equals a hundred yards off target there.

Inaccurate self-recognition is guaranteed to be off target when using the precision that is simple "child's toy" language. Indeed, language is the very key to handling intellect itself. Language is the very utensil that is used in the kitchen of experience (along with sensation, thought perception, and all the other raw ingredients) and turns intellect and the other separate gathered bits of information into knowledge. It is language that sifts through everything, measures out the portions, and bakes those disparate bits of information into solid knowledge.

It is language, and its precision, that allows oneself to recognize what an ingredient is in the first place.

Language must necessarily be precise (without any regard whatsoever to brevity) *EVEN* in the line of inquiry that *precedes* a patient's formulation of a *precise* answer. For example, if a patient is asked about a series of symptoms—"Do you have rebounding pain indicative of appendicitis?"—then such a question can't be precisely answered unless the patient's details explain what that pain is. Likewise, "Hey, you alive?" is equally going to lead to zero conclusive answers, obviously.

However, describing the exact nature of the pain ("sharp, rebounding") and in the right location (not just quadrant) could yield a reliably affirmative answer.

Thus, precision of *language* must *PRE*-exist even the line of questioning (in the case of CBT-introspection) or the introspection itself will be tainted by this fatal flaw.

11. Having to consciously pull my focus away from the meaning to instead consciously reform my words into "simpler language" reduces the actual meaning.

I AM REMINDED OF the analogy Julian Jaynes used in *The Origin of Consciousness in the Breakdown of the Bicameral Mind*. This will stick with you as it did me, and as it did him—playing piano (repeated from W. B. Carpenter's 1874 book, *Principles of Mental Physiology*).

Playing piano is an *un*conscious behavior. "A complex array of various tasks is accomplished all at once" with scarcely *ANY* consciousness of them whatsoever. Here's what the mind is doing:

1. Simultaneously reading two different lines of near hieroglyphics. (By the way, each line is in a different language from the other. The multi-note chords on top are in treble clef and the multi-note chords underneath are in bass clef—entirely different notes from each other.)

2. Each of these then is instantly and simultaneously translated.

3. Then the left hand is guided to perform one of the translated hieroglyphics while the right hand performs the other one.

4. Each finger (all ten) is then assigned to its own of various tasks, that fingering solving various motor problems, all without any awareness.

5. The mind interprets and adjusts on the fly the various sharps, flats, and naturals into black and white keys.

6. While obeying the timing of whole, half, quarter, dotted eighth, or sixteenth notes, rests and trills, crescendos and decrescendos, one hand perhaps in 3/4 time and the other in 4/4 or 6/8, while the feet (on pedals) are softening or slurring or holding various other notes.

All those things are done while the conscious side of the performer monitors and gauges the crowd or other instruments or is simply enjoying the musical rapture internally; the mind (consciousness) is elsewhere.

Now, instead, try to have that performer *explain* each task as he simultaneously reads it from the sheet music, in lieu of simply performing it.

He cannot do it, especially in real time.

Okay, well, can he explain each task (consciously retranslating his automatic tasks) into simple English as he performs it?

Again, impossible.

Having him verbally explain it forces his consciousness down into an unnatural language task instead of letting his fingers do the explaining. In other words, it forces him to articulate his thoughts, preventing him from playing. It destroys the intention of the "speech" (which, in this example, is best expressed through the language of music).

As we listen for the purpose of learning—that is, to understand the meaning of something—we are seldom ever conscious of the periods, commas, letters, syntax, or pronunciation. The phonemes disappear into words, the words into sentences, and the sentences disappear into meaning. In other words, what we catch through our listening skills is meaning.

The same is true with the production side. Try speaking with full consciousness of articulation and accent in a second language, or in one not as fluent as your primary. Make sure you get every accent and inflection perfect. Now using that, try to discuss any deep and spontaneous concept.

You can't do it. It is impossible.

Even as I write this, I am intent only on relaying the meaning, not whether or not I exceed the word count of the average reader's attention span. (My editor says to maintain a 19-word limit to a sentence.) Nor am I cognizant of each punctuation (until just now when I mentioned it—which, itself, slowed me down). I am not cognizant of the pressure on the pen or my posture. Only on the meaning. If I pull my attention away from the meaning I am trying to impart to instead focus on my posture, pen pressure etc., I lose some ability to deeply and precisely even *LOOK* at, or pull up, or create meaning—much less express that with precision.

Written and vocal speech are *NOT* mutually exclusive in this regard. Using another Jaynes analogy—a flashlight (conscious thought) can shine on only one thing.

III. Strictures on cognitive expression revises serious reporting bias.

A. What is reporting bias?

Let me explain. In my more immediate career (I left the hospital and the nursing field behind in 1995), I constantly clashed and fought with senior administrators and analysts to establish an atmosphere of non-reporting bias.

(A brief aside, it is baffling how no one in the BOP wonders why the larger DOJ record made sure there was a very long 18-year gap in my work history in the BOP files. None of you thought it was odd that there's a two-decade blank spot in my résumé according to BOP records? Really?!? That didn't strike you as odd?)

Reporting bias is a poison.

In my more relevant and recent career, it was important to develop, maintain, and constantly evaluate sources of information. Those of us who did this sort of work or facilitated it in any way sought out the best sources from the field that we could find—and constantly pressed those sources for measures of reliability (which we call the "degree of confidence"). This is all part of what we call the "intelligence cycle." The intelligence cycle has its minutiae within each stage or phase to which bias could play a major role, but for the purposes of keeping to the primary issue—I need not get bogged down into that—I can explain this concept just fine by using the longer macrocycle itself.

This is both dissimilar and yet still similar to the analogy I used earlier about monitoring the physiography and telemetry of patient Mrs. Smith and reporting it to her doctor with accuracy and precision.

Structurally, those of us in the field would compile a report, citing the hell out of our source (while simultaneously suggesting that we don't have 100% confidence in the source's reliability, just as kind of a CYA move, in case the source turned out to be totally wrong), including as many specific details as possible, sometimes including the methods used, and (if we felt bold enough) sometimes our own recommendations and analysis (both of which were routinely ignored).

All that (the full compilation) would then be sent to a reports officer (although these days they call this person something else). That RO is key. It is his, or just as often *her*, job to scrub the field report of sources and methods (redacting) and send it "cleaned up" to the analysts (who often ignore it).

The analyst would then take what the reports officer gave him (also often a *her*) and make sense of it, fit it with the known picture, and would often recommend a specific response or action based on the larger view. That analyst has multiple field (or "case") pipelines running to him.

Then the policy makers would decide on larger courses of action (or if necessary, specific actions), which would then be added to the workload of those in the field who already (generally) have very wide latitude and autonomy—or it would be delegated to a specialized team.

B. During my time, I burned through quite a lot of ROs because they would leave out my relevant details or overtly change the field analysis by subtly altering my tenor or tone.

Why did the reports officer do this?

Because of proximity and for the mere sake of pleasing the analysts. You see, ROs and analysts are in the same building. They are closer to each other, whereas the core collector of that information (i.e. the one in the field) is often thousands of miles away.

Often (very often) analysts have their own bent, their own viewpoint for which they have a bias. For *them*, everything must fit the predisposition of their existing corpus of solutions. In short—analysts are naturally analyst-centered.

All pegs must be round to make the analyst happy. Because of mere proximity, the analyst can more easily assert himself to the RO than can the person in the field. And so, they do. ("When you submit a report to me, I want it to be *THIS* way.")

C. But, all pegs aren't round. In fact, most pegs have their *OWN* shape.

1. Sometimes, the analyst has a particular bias simply because they know there is a *political* bias from the administration above. In fact, that is usually the case.

2. Rarely do the conditions on the ground exactly match the political bias of administrators, which pressures the analysts, who then simply "don't want to hear it" from the un-round pegs.

3. Therefore, the reports officer takes the field report and, in order to cater to the *linguistic* demands of the analyst, rounds off the peg. Then the analyst is given a nice round peg—a linguistically clean report.

   THAT report, however, *BECAUSE* of its alterations of language, is false.

D. For obvious reasons, such a thing can be catastrophic.

1. Complex matters (as most things are which require introspection or analysis) can *NOT* be treated as simple matters. Expression of the details (i.e. the complexity itself) *IS* part of the problem to solve and weigh.

2. Altering the language—that is, catering the syntax—by the RO changes the meaning. It is fundamental that language *IS* critical to meaning and that there is no such thing as meaning without proper understanding (even if it is communication with oneself).

   Quite often I returned to discover that the RO had changed or completely reversed the meaning or relevance of the original report. This catering to the analyst's whims caused me to reject quite a few ROs throughout the years. Sometimes this was after an absurd internal battle (in the bureaucratic sense), which I'd eventually win every single time, but the battles themselves were exhausting, politically damaging to careers (maybe even mine), and never should have been fought in the first place.

3. As the Dutschke Way was taught to others (and eventually became the standard), detailing and accurate reporting was insisted upon in order to ensure that the final decision-making was based upon the *ACTUAL* conditions on the ground as opposed to some operational bias from an altered meaning—or lost in translation due to reporting bias. No longer did the policy makers and various consumers of intel hear only what they wanted to hear. The final work product has to reflect the exact conditions (with the relevant details). If it does not, then the decided course of action will address something else, something different than the original issue.

   If I ask, "What day is it?" and you answer, "chocolate," then you've not addressed the issue. Thanks.

4. Reporting bias (catering language to the listener, not the speaker) affects the analysis and course of action *AND* the reevaluation of the issue. It is an unnecessary asininity which serves *NO* real propose and *NO* one's interest.

The parallel is that if you want me to use superficial language, then I can only address superficial issues. That is simply how thought itself works. Seriously. Try it for yourself. Grab a couple pieces of paper and write a two-page expression of how you currently believe your anxiety over the human condition affects potential sleep habits—but write it in Portuguese... or in Albanian ... or Finnish.

What's the problem?

You can't personally go that deep using that language? Why not? Limited vocabulary?

Exactly.

Thought itself, the ability to think, is dependent upon language as well as its expression. Depth of cognition and analysis is contingent upon depth of language.

I am *not* saying something revolutionary here. This is elementary-level understanding (ironically). I've been beaten to the punch (by centuries, even). Frege, Bertrand Russell, Wittgenstein, Saussure, George Edward Moore, Schlick, Vygotsky, Carnap, Ayer, Tarski, John Langshaw Austin. Even modern-day Chomsky. So, it baffles me that here in this environment, where introspective analysis is supposedly expected, I have *ANY* resistance at all to cognitive expression.

In fact, the idea that I *SHOULD* use imprecise language would certainly be characterized by Albert Ellis himself as a cognitive distortion. (I think it already fits several examples of all-or-nothing thinking.)

The argument that simpler (thus imprecise) language will "help others in the community help you" is an argument which holds no water. It is without merit or logic.

a. Reporting bias (aside from not preserving the precise meaning) involves *OTHERS'* ability to properly assess and analyze the real "conditions on the ground." Therefore, adversely affecting the accuracy of any solution (or in *THIS* case, "feedback from the community").

b. Reread a. above. It is the thrust of the problem. An obvious one.

c. It is also important that in reality, there is *NO* such thing as "the community." This very unit is comprised of individuals. Each individual is capable of understanding at their own individual level. Each is a fully autonomous thinking person. There is no such thing as "collective thought." Thus, it is impossible for each individual to see, understand, react to, or analyze in exactly and precisely the same manner. Nor *should* any diverse "community" wish for that. The diversity of perspective, cognition, and understanding can only be a strength if the objective isn't some lowest common denominator.

d. If only two out of 120 can follow or understand me on issue A, then those *two* may be qualified to help.

e. If I mention issue B, which would be understandable to everyone, then that (likely more superficial) issue B would be open to a greater number of individuals for feedback.

But really, should I be shooting for quality or quantity? The obvious, statement is that a shotgun approach is inappropriate when precision is called for. There may well be plenty of issues with which one might "struggle" (a *seriously* overused word here), and where a shotgun or surface-level approach is adequate. But that would be a very, very low bar for a test of CBT, wouldn't it?

CBT (over generalization alert!) is better than that.

I don't mean theoretically so. I mean currently as practiced. There are CBT modules for boundaries, trauma, car crashes, and other very specific therapies. Hell, there's even a CBT module for a lost pregnancy or miscarriage.

Very few pegs (in real life) are round.

And the deeper one looks, the less round they are.

Insisting upon an alteration of reporting syntax *IS* an obvious (self) reporting bias which helps no one. The only *honest* way to preserve the *integrity* of the reporting is to simply not impose strictures which would alter it.

Within the three phases of information being calculated (expressed, analysis, re-expression including feedback— that's really four phases if one counts implementation), if there is *ANY* weakness or ambiguity in the language at *ANY* phase, it impacts the precision of any subsequent phase as a structural matter.

IV. Metaphysical reality is cognitively expressed, but also is understood within the boundaries of language itself. Language *IS* reality.

A. What I mean is that the ontological and metaphysical reflections (expressed and understood as language) necessarily prefaces the very quantificational logic of each and every phase of cognitive calculations, down to each detail within each phase.

It actually *PREFACES* the need to calculate anything in the first place, since the inaugurate event which begins or renews any cycle or phase of information exchange or calculation is most often a trigger of someone else's expression (language). That is exemplified by this very sentence. Before you even have an opportunity to consider calculating or understanding the very statement I just made, I had to express it or make it. My thought—expression of cognition—is the trigger for whatever it is you think of it. Thus, my quality and precision in that trigger, in part, dictates your response.

B. The *full* meaning of everything and anything is entirely and inherently dependent upon the thoughts and deductive tools available as language itself. That is, the compositionality of meaning can *ONLY* reach as far as language can go.

Cognition and language are inalienable companions. (This is particularly so with any logical analysis of intangible concepts such as thoughts, feelings, and attitudes.)

Deductive reasoning can only be attempted derivatively of the syntax used in the functional expression. Meaning (or an individual's understanding of it) is downstream from language since a person's understanding of metaphysical concepts is defined by that individual's ability to define anything in the first place. Defining anything is an exercise in language as much as anything else.

(An equation can only be worked out to solvability when correct and accurate numbers are properly plugged into their requisite and corresponding places.)

C. The relationship between thought and language is intractable and uncompromisable for another reason, very similar. That is this: A thought (itself) is not complete *UNTIL* it is expressed to its fullness.

1. Meaning flows from thought. Meaning cannot be divorced from the activities and behavior of the language user.

   Now this may seem counterintuitive to superficial thinkers. Indeed, first instinct is to insist that thought precedes expression—that expression flows *FROM* thought. On the surface, this would appear obviously true. But not so.

2. As Albert Ellis postulated (and this CBT progeny teaches), it is actually cognition itself that is downstream from expression.

This program generally based on CBT principles suggests and teaches that altering the *expression* will, over time, alter perspective—therefore "changing" cognition (even self-defeating cognition).

3. As this applies to the "listeners," if they cannot help me at the level of expressing or analyzing, then they will try to "fix" me at some *OTHER* level—"fixing" problems that I don't have and have not expressed. Obviously, this is not helpful. Worse, still, it is counterproductive for *everyone*.

   A person (where a "community" is comprised of individual persons) only hammering at things within his easy reach will hammer everything in sight, missing those things which actually require some degree of mental reach.

   I greatly doubt that staff here would consider that stifling cognition and analysis is a prerequisite for CBT. Quite the opposite.

4. Expression *DRIVES* cognition.

   And those who are *richer* in expression are capable of deeper analysis as a matter of causality, not corollary coincidence.

   Abstract concepts are complex by nature. Thus, the inter-definition of any exploration requires equally complex language. That is an inarguable axiom. While people may share a language, the expression by any person is an individual predicate, a system that is structurally unique as well.

   (Personal note: There is a well-known and well-studied

phenomenon about prisoners that the constant downward pressure of the environment itself arrests, and to a degree even regresses, social development. A boy who is only 16 and who is in such a downward-pressure environment and never emerges from it will likely *stay* at *that* level of maturity. I suggest the same is true of their intellect as well. Prison is generally *NOT* an environment which fosters normal growth.)

5. Linguistic determination is so much a part of cognitive development that both the inter-psychological *AND* intra-psychological calculations are part of the conceptual theme that superimposes over metaphysical reality (redundant) itself.

   Thought is actually reconstructed *AS* it is being transformed into speech (spoken or written). Thought, and the ability to express it, are so inexorably intertwined that perception and analysis is conceptually dependent on thought, and vice versa.

6. The classic example of this is how disparate cultures (with dissimilar languages) actually process and compute (think) differently, such as the often cited example of our English word for "snow."

   To us English speakers, "snow" is "snow." That's it. However, the Inuit people ("Eskimo" tribes) utilize many different words for what we know of as only "snow." The Inuit make many sometimes very fine-tuned distinctions about that which we call and understand as "snow" that to them cannot be so conflated.

> They actually perceive and see those variants differently. They, perceive, see, analyze, and describe those subtle differences in snow that others simply do not. The defining language isn't only expressed in vocal speech, but in their own heads.

The model typified here in this residential unit forces the presumption that we are dealing with mentally impaired oafs who are too stupid to understand anything. I contend that presumption causes greater harm than good. In fact, it inflicts harm itself, as it is a downward pressure which obstructs the deeper introspection we should encourage.

If we only treat these people as though they are stupid prisoners, they will adapt themselves to conform with that costume.

In Summary

So, while there may exist some norms of representation through common tautological propositions using a common syntax, logical syntax which accurately describes exact meaning provides the only methodology to set out the properties of *ANY* meaningful proposition—it *enhances* the ability to be fully understood. This is the case no matter what that proposition is—complex abstract conceptualization, self-analysis, or even "feedback."

Because syntactic precision is necessary to delineate between complex abstract structural relationships and empirical or cognitive content, we shouldn't *fear* or shun the meta-language which preserves that clarity and truth (in either the analytical, reporting, or feedback stage). In fact, we should embrace it when it happens and should teach it as time, ability, and circumstance allows.

Therefore, this proposal seeks the very reasonable compromise. The compromise is simply that I (Dutschke) be given the license to fully express (without ridicule) within my own discretion whatever needs to be expressed at the appropriate level of syntax as is required to meet that level. If the issue is but superficial and vague, then I'll strive to not overcomplicate any simple matter.

But not all matters are simple. Deeper analysis demands deeper language. Not all psychological pegs are round (most aren't, by nature).

In short, I simply propose that I be allowed to speak as deeply as the issue being addressed is. This is, I feel, quite reasonable and is the standard of practice for psychotherapy anyway. If there are any objections to this reasonable solution (to a problem I feel never should have existed in the first place) or if there is *any* disagreement at all with the underlying premises outlined so far, then I would love to hear them.

I'm not looking for debate (or even confirmation), but I am not closed from hearing any rational opposing convictions, if there is room for any to exist.

I'll close with this: If we are expected not to criticize or impugn other individuals whose speech is hampered (either by their limited grasp of the English language or by their limited cognition), then this expectation should work both ways. Why should my ability to express myself not be equally inoculated against that very same criticism?

CBT cannot be imprecise.

If we are not to teach precision here to those who need it, then what are we doing?

OTHER BOOKS BY J. EVERETT DUTSCHKE

The Perfect Weapon

How God Does It

Dead Wrong

B.B. Quincy and the Giant Kraken

B.B. Quincy and the Minotaur

B.B. Quincy and the Green Dragon

B.B. Quincy and the Cyclops

www.ingramcontent.com/pod-product-compliance
Lightning Source LLC
Chambersburg PA
CBHW022045050726
47591CB00003B/961

* 9 7 8 1 7 3 5 9 8 0 3 4 8 *